April Lee

New York

Published in 2013 by The Rosen Publishing Group, Inc.
29 East 21st Street, New York, NY 10010



Book Design: Michael Harmon

Photo Credits: Cover © iStockphoto.com/KenWiedemann; p. 4 © iStockphoto.com/CEFutcher; p. 5 Jeff Hutchins/Getty Images News/Getty Images; p. 6 atielense/Shutterstock.com; p. 7 Stephanie Frey/Shutterstock.com; p. 8 Sergej Khakimullin/Shutterstock.com; p. 9 Mat Hayward/Shutterstock.com; p. 10 © iStockphoto.com/bowdenimages; p. 11 © iStockphoto.com/sjlocke; p. 12 © iStockphoto.com/DonaldBowers; p. 13 © iStockphoto.com/kirin_photo; p. 14 Bob Pool/Photographer's Choice/Getty Images; p. 16 Cardaf/Shutterstock.com.

ISBN: 978-1-4488-8941-9
6-pack ISBN: 978-1-4488-8942-6

Manufactured in the United States of America

CPSIA Compliance Information: Batch #WS12RC: For further information contact Rosen Publishing, New York, New York at 1-800-237-9932.

Word Count: 88

# Contents

We live in a town.

There are many ways to get around our town.

They walk to the playground.

She walks to the playground.

He rides his bike to the store.

They ride their bikes to the store, too.

She rides the bus to school.

They ride the bus to school, too.

He rides in a car to go to the movies.

They ride in a car to go to the library.

There are many ways to get around town.
How do you get around where you live?

# Getting Around Town

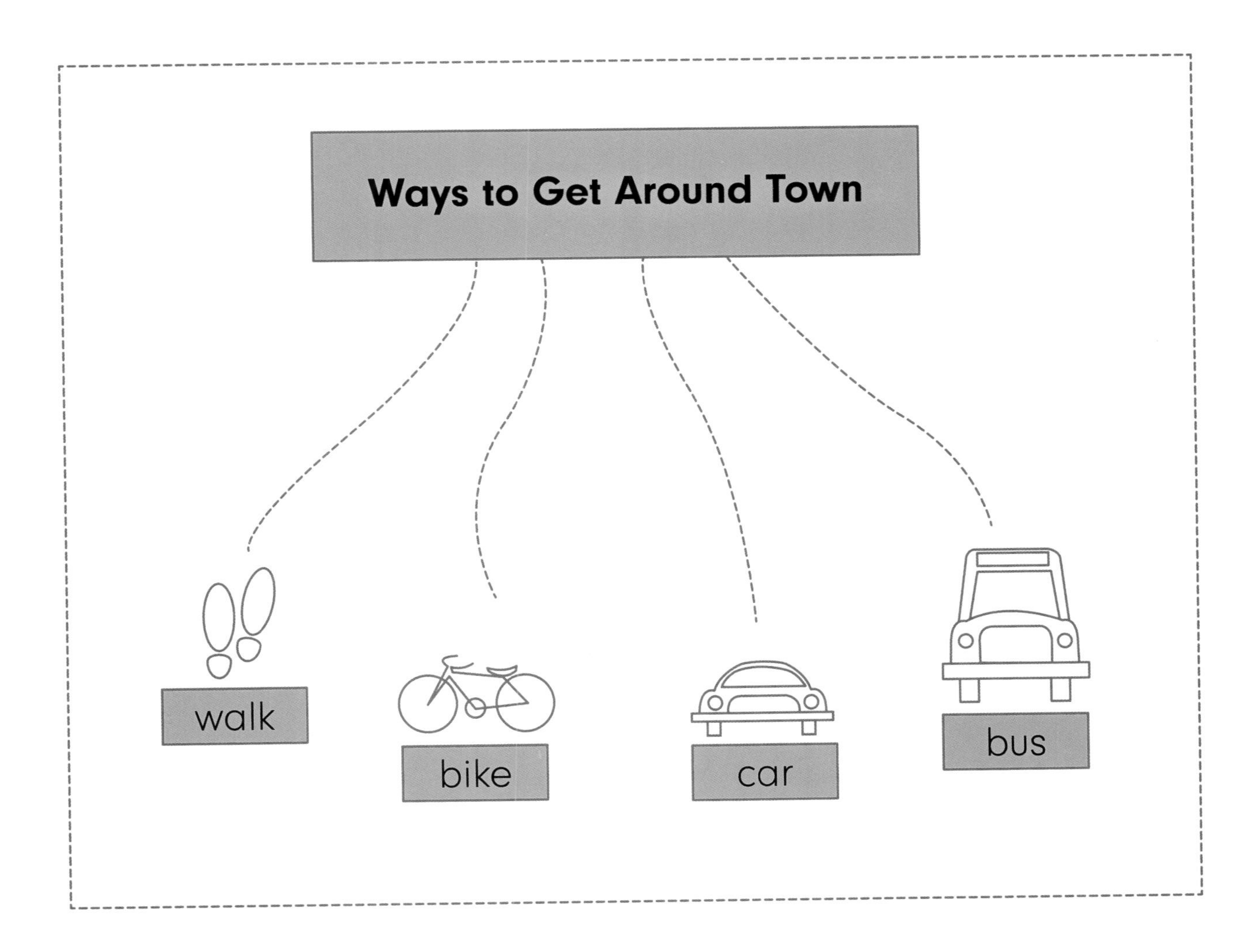

# Words to Know

bike

bus

car

playground

# Index